The Young World Library is a series designed for the
young reader. The stories are taken from some of the
world's best-known novels, plays, legends, operas and
ballets. They have been simplified and re-told in a way
which keeps close to the spirit of the original, while bringing
everything within the immediate grasp of the young
reader's understanding of words. Equally important are
the illustrations, which have been chosen both to delight
the eye and to match the special character of each story.
Thus the Young World Library offers young readers a
unique stepping stone towards the use and enjoyment of
books. It also introduces them in a lively, up-to-date way
to many famous stories and characters from the
wonderful world of literature and the performing arts.

Series Editor: Alan Blackwood

Cover design by Hildegarde Bone

© 1973 Thomas Nelson & Sons Limited
S.B.N. 72380962 3
Printed in Great Britain by A. Wheaton & Co., Exeter

PROSPERO'S MAGIC ISLAND

Adapted and told by
Anne Webb

Illustrated by
Hildegarde Bone

Based on the play *The Tempest* by
William Shakespeare

NELSON
YOUNG WORLD

Thunder crashed, lightning flashed and the wind howled through the rigging of the tiny ship. The passengers were panic-stricken as the waves crashed against the side and sent spray all over the deck.

And they were very important passengers, too. There was Alonso, the King of Naples, his son Ferdinand, and various courtiers and servants.

The boatswain tried his best to control the ship under these rough conditions. But he was hampered by the passengers who came on deck and tried to interfere. He rudely ordered them to go below, but they refused and the King prayed in vain to calm the storm.

The storm got worse,
and panic took hold of everyone.
As the ship foundered, Gonzalo,
the King's old counsellor,
commented, *"The wills above be
done! But I would fain die a dry
death."* And then everyone
abandoned ship and swam
towards a nearby island.

The storm had not been a
natural one. It had been raised
by a magician who lived on
the island.

His name was Prospero and
he had a lovely young daughter
called Miranda. She had
watched the shipwrecking with
horror. But her father was a
merciful man and had made sure
that no one would die in the
tempest. He had arranged to
guide them to the island for a
very special purpose of his own.

Twelve years ago Prospero
had been Duke of Milan. His
wicked brother; Antonio, had
plotted with the King of Naples to
overthrow him.

Antonio had seized power and had Prospero, with the three-year-old Miranda, set adrift at sea in an old boat without mast, rig or tackle. He had intended that they should perish, but Gonzalo, the old nobleman, had put food and clothing into the boat for them. And so it was that they had drifted to this island.

And now, as a result of Prospero's magic, the King of Naples and Antonio, now the Duke of Milan, had come to this island.

Prospero had a fairy-like servant called Ariel.

The only other person living there was Caliban. He was the son of a witch and was a crawling, animal-like creature.

Prospero had taught Caliban to speak and encouraged him to live with them and be their servant.

But Caliban was not grateful. In return for Prospero's kindness, he had once tried to attack Miranda. So, from that day onwards, Caliban was kept as a slave, his violent temper kept under control by the power of Prospero's magic. Caliban had become a very sullen creature, always looking for ways of getting his revenge on Prospero.

Ariel, on the other hand, was a light, airy creature. He was always cheerful and good-tempered and anxious to serve and please Prospero.

Prospero had given Ariel the job of bringing the survivors of the shipwreck ashore.

Ferdinand was feeling very miserable. He thought that he was the only one on the island and that his father must have perished in the tempest.

Prospero had a special plan in mind concerning Ferdinand and he asked Ariel to go and fetch him. Ariel made himself invisible and went to find Ferdinand.

Ariel charmed Ferdinand into following him by the beauty of his singing.

Ariel's song comforted and reassured:

"Full fathom five thy father lies;
Of his bones are coral made;
Those are pearls that were his eyes,
Nothing of him that doth fade,
But doth suffer a sea-change
Into something rich and strange.
Sea-nymphs hourly ring his knell:
Hark! now I hear them—
Ding-dong bell."

Ariel led Ferdinand, as Prospero had ordered, within sight of the sleeping Miranda. It was Prospero's plan that the two should fall in love and marry, so that the breach between Prospero and Ferdinand's father Alonso, could be healed.

Miranda had never seen a man, apart from her father and Caliban, in the whole of her life. As Ferdinand approached, led by the invisible Ariel, Prospero wakened his daughter. To Miranda, Ferdinand seemed like a god, a "thing divine". And Ferdinand fell in love with her at first sight, as Prospero had intended. But Prospero did not want their love to blossom too quickly, and he also wanted Ferdinand to prove his love for Miranda.

So Prospero pretended to be
displeased and to distrust
Ferdinand. He accused him of
being a spy. He took the young
man prisoner:

> *"I'll manacle thy neck*
> *and feet together*
> *Sea water shalt thou drink."*

Poor Miranda could not
understand her father's strange
behaviour.

Ariel soon had to be busy in another part of the island. The King and his courtiers were bemoaning their fate and the loss of Ferdinand. Ariel put them all to sleep with the exception of Sebastian, Alonso's brother, and Antonio. Antonio persuaded Sebastian that this was his chance to kill his brother, the King, and seize the throne for himself.

Sebastian agreed and it was decided that Antonio would attack the King. Gonzalo would be killed, too, and Sebastian would take care of him. They were confident that the rest of the courtiers would take orders from anyone and do as they were told.

"*They'll take suggestions as a cat laps milk,*" they said.

The two conspirators drew their swords to commit the murder and cautiously crept up on the King and his old counsellor.

But Ariel had been keeping watch. The murderers were just going to strike when Ariel started to sing in Gonzalo's ear. Gonzalo woke up at once and found Antonio and Sebastian with their swords drawn.

Gonzalo's startled shout
awakened the King who was
puzzled to see Antonio and
Sebastian with their swords
drawn. The conspirators did not
know what to do.

They made up a story about
having heard some fierce wild
animals. The King believed them.
Then he said that a search should
be started at once for Ferdinand.

Meanwhile Caliban was cursing
his master, Prospero.
*"All the infections that the
sun sucks up
From bogs, fens, flats, on Prospero
fall and make him
By inch-meal a disease!"*

Then Caliban saw Trinculo
approaching. Trinculo was the
King's jester and had come
ashore with the rest of the
court party.

Caliban had never seen
anyone wearing such strange
clothes. Trinculo's suit was made
up of many different colours,
and his cap had bells on it.

Caliban, thinking that this must
be a servant of Prospero
coming to check up on him, tried
to hide. He laid down flat and
pulled his cloak over his head.

Coming upon this strange
object with the mis-shapen
feet sticking out from
under the cloak, Trinculo was
puzzled. He could not make out
what it was.

But then he noticed that the sky
was overcast and the rain was
threatening to *fall by pailfuls*
so there was nothing for him to do
but crawl under Caliban's cloak
for shelter. His feet stuck out from
the cloak too.

At that moment, the King's
butler, Stephano, arrived. He had
found a full cask of wine and had
become quite drunk.

When he saw the cloak with four feet sticking out from under it, he thought he had found some strange animal.

He started to inspect the "animal", pulling a leg out here, punching and kicking there. Eventually Stephano uncovered Caliban's head and insisted on giving him a drink. And then he recognised Trinculo's voice. He pulled him out from under the cloak by his legs. Trinculo was delighted to be reunited with his old friend and insisted on dancing round with him.

After Caliban had drunk
more of Stephano's wine, he
became as tipsy as Stephano.
Then he thought that Stephano
must be some kind of a god. He
was quite ready to fall down at
his feet and worship him. He
wanted to serve him, thinking he
would then be free of Prospero
forever.

Caliban made up a song which
he sang happily:
  " 'Ban, 'Ban, Ca-Caliban,
Has a new master—Get a new man."
    In the meantime, Prospero
had put Ferdinand to work
carrying logs. He had ordered
him to erect a large pile of them
before sunset. But Ferdinand did
not grumble about the task. He
saw it as a way of proving his love
for Prospero's daughter.

When she was sure that her
father was safely in his study,
Miranda crept out to join
Ferdinand.

Ferdinand asked Miranda
her name, so that he could
mention it in his prayers.
Miranda, in turn, asked
Ferdinand if he loved her and he
swore by everything he could
think of that he did.

Miranda told Ferdinand that
although she felt unworthy of his
love, she would be his wife if he
would have her. And, of course,
Ferdinand quickly agreed.

Unbeknown to the two
lovers, Prospero had been
listening. He was delighted with
what he heard, but left Ferdinand
to get on with his work.

Stephano had been having difficulty in controlling his new servant, Caliban. Caliban could think of nothing but killing and eventually persuaded Stephano and Trinculo to set out on an expedition to murder Prospero. Caliban said they must destroy Prospero's magic books first so that the old man would be quite helpless.

Ariel, still wearing his invisible cloak had heard the conversation. He confused everyone by mimicking voices and interrupting the speakers.

But Caliban did manage to tell Stephano about Miranda, who then decided that he would be king of the island, and have Miranda as his queen.

Ariel at once flew back to tell
Prospero what was going on.
Meanwhile, Prospero had been
arranging a rich banquet for the
royal party in another part of
the island. But as soon as the
courtiers approached the banquet,
it vanished from sight.

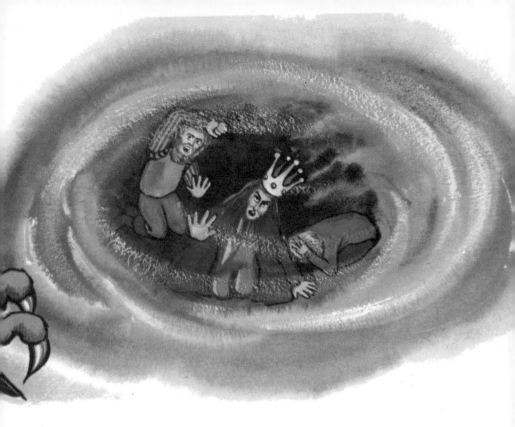

And then Ariel appeared
disguised as a hideous monster
with a woman's face and the
claws and wings of a bird. He
spoke in a threatening way to
the three men who had once
tried to destroy Prospero and
frightened them greatly.

Prospero had prepared a
wonderful wedding feast for his
daughter and Prince Ferdinand.
He used his magic to bring to
earth the three goddesses,
Ceres, Iris and Juno.

Prospero knew that the time
was now coming for him to leave
the island and return to the
world of men, as the Duke of
Milan.

He would leave all his magic
behind him on the island.
"I'll break my staff,
Bury it certain fathoms in the earth,
And deeper than did ever
plummet sound,
I'll drown my book."
But Prospero still had to deal
with Caliban and his companions,
for Ariel had warned him of
their plans.

To delay the conspirators, Ariel led them through rough, thorny country and into a slimy dirty pond. And then Prospero brought up a pack of spirits in the form of hounds who chased Caliban and his terrified companions.

Next, Prospero put on the clothes that he had worn when he was the Duke of Milan, twelve years earlier, and he summoned the royal party to him.

Everyone recognised him at once
and they were all very sorry
about what they had done. But
Prospero was forgiving towards
them all.

He pointed to Ferdinand who
was sitting in a nearby cave,
playing chess with Miranda.
Alonso was overjoyed to find his
son alive and well, and even
more delighted when he heard
that he was going to marry
Miranda.

Then Ariel brought in Caliban, Stephano and Trinculo. They were feeling very sorry for themselves. Caliban at once went back to work for Prospero with the conviction that he had behaved like a *"thrice-doubled ass"*.

Then Prospero invited Alonso and the rest of his court to his home.

There he told them all about his adventures on the island during the past twelve years.

In the meantime Ariel had been very busy making preparations for Prospero's return home. He had fortunately kept the ship and its crew safe with his magic powers and soon everyone was aboard and it was ready to sail.

Ariel's last task for Prospero
was to ensure calm seas for the
homeward voyage.

When the ship had set sail,
Caliban and Ariel were alone
again upon the island. Ariel
composed a lovely song to tell of
the delights of freedom:

"Where the bee sucks, there suck I,
In a cowslip's bell I lie
There I couch when owls do cry.
On the bat's back I do fly
After summer merrily.
Merrily, merrily shall I live now
Under the blossom that hangs
on the bough."